Scarecrow

The Inner Circle Series #2

Kailin Gow

AUTHOR'S NOTE

Thank you for picking up Scarecrow, the second book in the Inner Circle Series.

This series is a New Adult Dark Romance and contains dark themes that may have some triggers. Recommended for 18+.

Scarecrow (The Inner Circle #2)

Summary

Parker James killed his father, one of the founders and kingpins in the Inner Circle.

Now his son, groomed to replace the father in the Inner Circle, and trained to be an assassin will seek revenge.

He is known as the Scarecrow.

Perfect for Parker James. Having the Scarecrow after him will get him closer to Oz.

But now the other players, including Dorothy, The Wizard, and the Lion's coming out to play, too.

**The Inner Circle Series is a Dark College Romance Thriller with lots of action, steamy scenes, language, and twists and turns. Recommended for age 18 and up.

Prologue

<u>Dante Black/Parker James</u>

I had no qualms taking out Stanley, the first hit I went after from the Inner Circle.

While I had done a lot of dirty jobs for all the members of the Inner Circle, Stan was the worst. He always had someone that he wanted taken out.

Here was the man who had sent me to kick a guy's head in because the poor guy had infringed on Stan's territory.

Here was the man who had made me kill a fifteen year old kid who had stupidly dared to stand up to Stan when I was just fifteen years old. The only reason Stan wanted him dead was to prove a point. His way of telling all the other guys out there not to fuck with him.

Stanley knew I had a mechanical heart. He knew I was cold. He knew that I had no empathy for my victims. He knew that snapping a man's neck was no different to me than snapping a twig.

But I also knew that Stanley, like all the five Founders of the Inner Circle, including my own father, had trained his own offspring to become an assassin, just like I had been trained and groomed since childhood. I knew, like I was trained, to avenge the very parent who was a Founder. It was the assurance the Founders had against each other in case they ever went against each other. There will be revenge, and it would be from a very well-trained assassin who took the hit very personally.

So, I knew, Stanley's offspring would be going after me soon. What I didn't know was who the offspring was besides his Code Name. All I knew was that he was given a name that was part of the storybook, The Wizard of Oz, just like I had. My Code Name was Tin Man.

And he was the Scarecrow.

Now I not only had to carry out my mission to eliminate the rest of the Founders of the Inner Circle, who had killed my father and ordered the death of me, along with my former assignment and target… Summer Jones, the girl who stole my heart; but I had to do it as soon as possible, before I get eliminated by the Scarecrow, and also the other offsprings of the Founders, who by now, were tipped off to what was going on.

I picked up my phone to give Ace, my assistant - a thief and hacker whom I had saved from the cartel, and was now only a handful of people who knew me as being the former Dante Black and now Parker James – a heads up.

"Hey, what's up, Boss?" Ace asked in his casual laid back style.

"Now that one of the Founders is dead, the other three would be tipped off and on high alert. They're going to be sending the rest of the Offsprings at us. Stanley's own son, The Scarecrow, had already made an appearance, when Stanley's record company made the announcement that Stanley died in a tragedy, but the company's helm would go to his son, who will be releasing their newest record named The Scarecrow."

"It doesn't get clearer than that," Ace said. "So, what's the plan?"

"Come back to the Malibu house," I said. "Let's discuss it there. Nothing over the phone now. They may not know it was me, but they will begin tracing any contact Stanley had over the last couple of months."

"Gotcha," Ace said. "I'll stay off the phone with you on any I.C. or "Inner Circle" stuff."

"Good," I said. "I've got a plan, but it requires a lot of stealth, guts, and yeah, nuts. Think you can handle it?"

"I haven't back away from anything you've gotten me into before, have I?" Ace asked.

"No, good," I said.

"Yeah, after I learned how the I.C. had screwed up my life and my family's no matter how small our little mom and pop business was, I want to bring them down, too," Ace said. "Not to mention that they were responsible for the Cartel going after me, too."

"Yeah," I said. "That, too."

"So, yes, I'm in all the way," Ace said. "By-the-way, any idea who the Scarecrow is? Any of the Offsprings?"

"Good," I said. "No, I don't know the real identity of Scarecrow or the other Offsprings. It was always something that made my dad's role as the head of the Inner Circle at a disadvantage, just to prove his loyalty to the Inner Circle. My dad allowed my identity as Dante Black, his own son to be revealed to all in the Inner Circle, including their offspring, and to allow them to use me as their assassin, just to prove how good I was. How devoted my dad was to the organization that he gave his son completely over to its cause. Meanwhile, their offsprings were not known to Dad and me. The Inner Circle supposedly had offsprings and had trained them in their own way. Over the years, I've heard of some assignments they've been sent to do and had accomplished, but I never got cozy with any of them nor did I had the time to. I was busy doing

Inner Circle stuff, running my family's legitimate business, Black Biotech, and going to school. So, to answer your question about who the Offsprings are… I could only guess who, based on a few clues, but no, I didn't grow up knowing them at all."

"Well, then they could be anyone," Ace said. "Better keep our wits about us."

"Exactly," I said. "See you soon."

Chapter 1

<u>Parker James</u>
Malibu, CA

My Malibu mansion that Ace had found for me to fix up and fortified into a sort of fort with security cameras, sensors, a hidden room, and more felt pretty empty since Summer had to take off to visit her mother for a week. I had gotten used to her staying here with me, sharing my bedroom and bed with me almost every night.

Thank God that Ace had the wing on the opposite side of us so we could have all the privacy we needed. Summer had become a screamer, moaning so loudly, and fucking so passionately, it was as if she was another woman almost. Like she was putting on a show. While I loved the wild times we had in bed, something was off. Sex was supposed to be the most primal and instinctual act of a person, no matter how they remember it or knew what to do. In other words, you pretty much have sex the way you always do, amnesia or not.

Summer could not have changed that much after her amnesia, or could she?

While I fixed myself a drink and sat down in front of my computer, combing all the news articles on Stanley's death; Ace walked into my office, carrying a set of blueprints.

"What do you have there?" I asked.

"Blueprints on Rockefeller Real Assets' building in New York. You asked me to get you the blueprints a couple of days ago."

"Oh, yeah," I said. "Thanks," I took the blueprints and placed it aside.

"We're going after Rockefeller next, aren't we?" Ace asked. "The Founder who runs the world's real estate conglomerate."

"Yes, he's next. But then again, Worth, who runs the financial sector could be next, too," I said.

"Worth is based in Switzerland?" Ace asked.

"Last time I remembered, he is," I said. "Logistically, it would make sense to hit Rockefeller first and then go to Switzerland for Worth, but we don't have much time now that Stanley's been hit. They are all on to someone taking the Inner Circle out, and they will all be scrambling to do something about it."

"Well, it's a good thing I've scoured the dark web recently to find some black market stuff going on," Ace said. "I.C. stuff with signature huge purchases and transactions. Rockefeller has sold some of his real estate assets and had transferred a ridiculous amount into Swiss accounts."

"He's probably setting up shop in Europe," I said.

"So, let's go to Europe," Ace said.

"Hold on," I said, tapping into a computer I had planted surveillance in at Rockefeller Real Assets. I searched the emails on the computer along with the calendar. "Bingo! Your hunch was right. Rockefeller's planning on going to Switzerland this weekend. His secretary's made the arrangements."

"Worth is going to be there, too?" Ace asked.

"Looking at a few encrypted emails I just broke through, it looks like Worth and Rockefeller's meeting up to discuss I.C. stuff in Switzerland."

"We can get both of them at once," Ace said.

"That's my goal," I said. "Maybe Claire, too,"

"Claire?" Ace asked.

"Yes, the fifth Founder of I.C. She lives and operates out of France and runs the food and agriculture sector of the I.C." I said. "She's the only woman, but from what I remembered, she's far worst than the men when it comes to ruthlessness. She would kill her own offspring to get what she wants."

"Dang!" Ace said, "Brutal."

"I know. Dad's brutal and would have killed me, but he hesitated and that cost him his life. Claire wouldn't hesitate at all for anything. She's also known for enjoying the sufferings of others, just for kicks."

"Hope she's there at the I.C. party, too," Ace said, "Someone like her… the world wouldn't miss."

"Too bad I couldn't find any correspondence between her and the other I.C. founders from Rockefeller's assistant's computers even encrypted ones. She's smart not to even communicate through digital means these days."

"Carrier pigeons then?" Ace smiled.

"More like messengers," I said. "You never know who's going to be delivering the message. If you do remember who, though, it'll be the last time you see them because Claire would have the messenger killed just to keep everything secret, and to never have a loose end."

"Wow, that's ruthless alright," Ace said. "That's one woman you don't want to cross." He looked around and said, "Talking about woman, where's yours?"

"Summer said her mother is back from a mission so she is visiting with her this week at her mother's," I said.

Ace nodded. I could see him thinking about something, but haven't said anything yet.

"Spit it," I said. "What are you thinking?"

"Nothing," Ace said. "I know you've just re-found Summer and had rekindled your romance with her, so…"

"You don't like her being here with us?" I asked.

"Just that there's something off about her," Ace said. "I mean I know she had amnesia and all that, but sometimes I would catch her say something just to catch herself before she says more, like she's watching what she'll say. It's not a way most people act, you know?"

I nodded but didn't say anything.

"Just watch her," Ace said, "You know to see if it's a medical thing or something we should be looking out for."

"Sure," I said. "Now, let's get back to business. When can we take off for Switzerland?"

Ace took out his phone and started texting. "I just got a response."

"That was fast," I said.

"Yup, have a bunch of pilots and charters on speed-text, and one could be ready for us this afternoon at 5. We'll make it in time for lunch the next day."

"Great," I said, standing up. "Let's get packing."

Chapter 2

<u>Parker James</u>
Switzerland

"How do you do it?" Ace asked barely awake as I walked into his hotel suite next to mine. "How do you manage to look so bright and energetic after a flight like that and be ready for a full day's of work?"

"I slept on the plane, as you should've done," I said. "Refreshing and relaxing. Best sleep I always get is on these flights," I said.

"I took sleeping medicine, and drank some liquor, watched some boring news show… I just couldn't sleep like you," Ace said. "Now I'm paying the price."

I took one look at him and said, "Tell you what, you're no good for me or yourself when you're not 100 percent today. Stay here, get some sleep. I'm going to do some undercover work anyways. I should be able to get it done without a hitch."

Ace looked at me and wiped his eyes. "Oh no, you can't do it alone. I'll go take a shower, it'll wake me up. I'll be good to go in no time, Boss."

"Just be ready for backup, if you get my signal," I said. "That's all I need from you today. Rest up. Tomorrow's going to be a big day. Rockefeller's flying in, and today, I'm making sure we're ready to make it a memorial welcome for him."

"Right," Ace said. He got up and quickly set up his lap top, modem, and everything he needed. "I'll be monitoring you all the way, Boss."

"You're awake now?" I asked, handing him a large cup of coffee.

"I will be," he said, taking a big gulp of the coffee. "Like I said, a quick shower, coffee, and some energy drinks will get me going."

"Good," I said, picking up my small black tech bag and walking towards Ace's door. "You'll know when I'm in Worth's building when you start seeing a feed."

"Okay," Ace said. "I'll start going into their system now so I can shut down part of their security.

Give me about thirty minutes, and it should be ready."

"Perfect," I said. "See you later for dinner."

"Sure," Ace said. "The restaurant across from this hotel serves authentic Swiss food. Want to try that place?"

"Why not?" I asked.

"Good, something to look forward to," Ace said.

"Yup," I said, heading out.

"Be careful," Ace said. "I don't want to lose my job with you, Boss. So you better be around…"

I smiled. The 19 year-old kid was growing on me.

*****

Dressed like a sophisticated Swiss businessman, I walked through the hotel, blending in with the rest of the businesspeople there for a convention. It made the cover for our trip easy, and our location near Worth's headquarters convenient.

As soon as I was out the door of the hotel, I headed to a taxi cab to take me to a car rental where I picked up a small black van. Plastering the sides of the van with a logo for a telecom repair company, that matched the jacket I had changed into, which matched my cap, I was ready to pull up to the front gate of the Worth building.

"Hi," I said. "Doing some repair work," I said in German.

"Do you have authorization?" the security guard asked.

I pulled out a work order, on my repair company's letterhead and said, "This came about thirty minutes ago. A Ms. Guther called to have us come out to fix the telephone system wiring. Your internet's down, too? I'll take a look at it."

"Good, good," the security guard said, "Yeah, our internet is down. We are having a hard time connecting from our post out here to the head of security's office in the building."

"I'll work on all that when I get in," I said.

He waved me in and pointed for me to park in the spot closest to the entrance.

I parked my black van and made my way in, tipping my cap at the blonde buxom young woman who greeted me in the lobby. "So happy you are here," she said, smiling at me, while taking in my muscular body that made my jacket and slacks a bit

25

too tight. "I'll show you the way to our main control room," she said.

"You are not only very lovely," I said, "but so helpful, indeed."

She giggled. "My pleasure." She walked slightly in front me, swaying her ample hips that filled out her thin tight blue dress. "Call me Anna. I am the Head Secretary at Worth Global Financials. I know everyone and everything here."

"So remarkable for someone who young and sexy," I said, licking my lips.

Her eyebrows cocked up, and she looked down at my crotch. "Maybe after you fix our lines, I can help fix your problem."

"That would be nice," I said with my wicked grin. I took her hand to the front of my crotch to palm my hard-on. "That would be very nice indeed."

She looked hungrily at me and then her eyes went down to my crotch. "I love eating long large sausages. The bigger the better."

"I'm in heaven," I smiled. "Let me finish up with this first, and then you can take me somewhere…"

"My boss is away for a long lunch today," Anna said. "We can use his office."

"Sure," I said. "Your boss is?"

"Samuel Worth."

"Samuel Worth's own secretary?" I asked.

"Yes," she said.

"But you're far too young and lively to be his secretary," I said.

"For his purpose, I am just right," Anna said, looking pointedly into my eyes.

"Ahh, I see," I said. "You must be very talented."

Anna smiled. "You will see."

Chapter 3

Parker James

Less than half an hour later, I was in Samuel Worth's personal office, sitting at his desk, being sucked by Anna's talented mouth.

As her head bobbed up and down, I placed a pen with a hearing device in a cup full of pens on his desk. "Oh, that's good," I said, encouraging Anna to keep sucking on my dick, "really good." I pushed her head down lower as I positioned a microcamera along the edge of the side of his desk, hidden along the ledge. It would give Ace and me a good view of whoever came into Worth's office.

Anna kept going, and I was letting her mouth ride on me. Then her throat loosen, and I felt my dick slide down further. Fuck, she was deep-throating me.

It felt so good. I let go, letting my stress unleashed as she sucked me dry.

Afterwards, I kissed her forehead and said, "You are very talented, Anna. Very."

She smiled at me as I zipped up my pants. "And you are very well-hung, just like I like it. I love your dick. I love sucking on it so much. You live around here? Perhaps I can visit you at your place or you can come to my house. I don't live too far from work."

I patted her head and said, "I would love that very much, Beauty. Yes, if I can visit you at your house, I'll return the favor."

She looked like she almost climaxed then. "Here is my home address." She wrote down her address and phone number on the back of Worth's business card she had taken from his desk, and said, "Now I'll walk you out."

I drove the rented black van back to the rental car office, after taking off my fake logo and changed back into my business suit. After the cab dropped me off, I headed up to my suite, took a shower and changed before heading over to Ace's suite.

"Hello?" I said, walking in as he sat with two laptops opened in front of him.

He laughed. "I don't know how you do it, Boss. You not only set up the place so we have access to their computers, telephones, security; but you got a hell of a blowjob from it too!"

"Oh you heard my exchange with Anna?" I asked.

"Yes, and then some. That pen mic was clear and functioning perfectly. I heard every suck, every panting, man, she was going down on you like…" he gulped. "I was getting penis envy. Wished I can get some action like that once in a while."

"You might get lucky. Anna invited me to come over to her house for more. Who knows if she's open for more as in more than just one guy."

"Lucky her, if she is," Ace said. "Double the action."

"She's Worth's personal secretary. Has access to many things, including secrets, I'm sure. She's someone we should get to know much better, don't you think?" I asked.

"Definitely," Ace said. "Definitely. Like now is a good time. Worth just walked into his office."

I went over to watch the footage the microcamera was picking up in Worth's office. He was a man with grey hair and a large frame in his late fifties. And he was already unbuckling his belt to slide his pants down as he bent Anna over to fuck her from behind.

"Damn," Ace said, watching the old man bang the woman who had just given me head. "He's an animal."

"No wonder she prefers men like me," I said. "After that disgusting thing banging into her like that, any man would be better."

"Definitely," Ace said, watching the footage like it was some big game event. "Wait, they're done. And now he's asking her questions."

"Oh?" I asked, now interested. Would she mention me to her boss? And how?

"Anything interesting happened while I was at lunch, Anna?" Worth was saying.

"Just the usual. Nothing much," she said.

"Good," he said, patting her butt as he pushed her away. "No news is good news. Now go away. I have to get on the phone."

Anna walked dejectedly out of Worth's office.

"Well, that's certainly not a satisfying sexual experience for her," Ace said.

"I'm sure she's wishing for more," I said. "Now turn the volume up. I want to hear what Worth is saying on his phone call."

"So you think you're next on the list?" Worth was saying, "That's a given. We are all next. First Clay, then Stan. We are all falling one by one. Soon none of the Founders will be around. What are you going to do about it?"

I looked over at Ace as I waited for Worth to continue talking.

"Stan's son has already been dispatched. He is combing the Hollywood area where his father was murdered. He's a sly one…that Scarecrow. Almost as good as Dante Black, but not quite. Rob, the Scarecrow, grew up with my kid, the Wizard and also Claire's kid, Dorothy. They're friends, which Dante was never a part of because he was so isolated by Clay. If there's any weakness in the next generation of Inner Circle founders, it's their bond, their friendship. Scarecrow is soft on Dorothy. Best friends with my kid like brothers."

I waited again for Worth to continue speaking while Ace handed me some potato chips. "I'm starved, but this…"

"We can order room service," I said. "Save the restaurant next door for another meal. This is good stuff."

"Okay," Ace grabbed the room service menu and began ordering. "I know what I want. Been looking at the menu all day. What do you want, Boss?"

"The steak," I said. "You know how I like it."

"Sure," Ace said.

"You'll be in town tomorrow, Rock," Worth started saying. "To discuss how to handle this assassin. Good. Claire sent word to me the other day that her daughter Dorothy thinks Dante Black's alive and not dead as we all thought he was. Yeah, that Dorothy is as ruthless as her mother. More beautiful now too, after her plastic surgery complete makeover. She looks like a playboy centerfold now, the kind who lives on the beach in Southern California. Yeah, she's still keeping her disguise to root out that traitor Dr. Jones. She has everyone fooled. Everyone thinks Dorothy is Dr. Jones' daughter. Sunny Jones or what's her name…"

Ace looked over at me and I almost dropped the bag of potato chips in my hands.

What the Fuck?

"I thought something was up with this new Summer," Ace said.

My heart had plummeted to the ground as I realized all this time, the girl I thought was Summer, was not Summer at all, but Dorothy, an Assassin from the Inner Circle and Claire's daughter.

Chapter 4

<u>Parker James</u>

"Holy shit!" Ace said. "Summer was not your Summer, wasn't she?"

"To think I let Dorothy into our house, our fortress, with access to our information," I said.

"Luckily, you had all your computers and Dante Black stuff hidden in a secret room there, but what if she had been snooping. If she is Dorothy, she's a highly-trained assassin. She would know where to look, wouldn't she?" Ace asked.

"Fucking shit!" I said, picking up the computers and closing them shut. "Pack up. Pack up. Put everything away. We've got to move now."

"Why?" Ace asked.

"I texted Summer, um, I mean Dorothy where we were staying in Switzerland after I left Worth's building. I thought she should know in case of some emergency. Plus I was worried for her safety. Scarecrow would be out there looking for her, too."

"But she's not Summer," Ace said. "But Dorothy so…that assassin is probably on her way out…"

Ace was already putting all of his equipment into his suitcase, shoving his clothes into a bag, and getting his jacket on. "Head on out first and get us a car," I said.

I rushed across the suite to my room and quickly packed my suitcase. I was hoping Summer/Dorothy would not figure out I was Dante Black, but knowing how we I.C. Offsprings were trained to think, she would eventually figure it out. I was hoping she would figure it out later, rather than now.

I took out my gun and was prepare to shoot, if I saw her.

I was about to head out of my room when I heard a familiar voice. "Room service!"

It was sweet and feminine. Just like she had practiced it to be… just like Summer's voice.

Damn, Dorothy was here already.

When the room across from her didn't open, I heard a shotgun fire and from the peephole, I saw long caramel hair flying as a woman headed into the suite Ace had been in with me just minutes before.

I had given Ace my suite, switching it with his since it had a better reception. So Dorothy thought I was in that suite. Good thing Ace had left already, and as soon as I saw Dorothy entered his suite, I flew out of mine and ran down the hallway to the stairwell.

We were only on the third floor of the hotel so it didn't take long for me to reach the ground floor. I heard the door to the stairwell open and Summer/Dorothy's voice shouting out, "Are you there Dante Black? Are you? If you are, know that the Scarecrow, the Lion, the Wizard, and I are out to get you!"

The door of the stairwell slammed shut as I ran out through the lobby to the front of the hotel where Ace was waiting in a cab. I hopped in and shouted for the driver to hurry.

He started the car, and had driven past the entrance and out to the road just as I caught a glimpse of Summer, um, Dorothy running out of the hotel, wearing a red trench coat and carrying a shotgun.

"My gosh," Ace said, "That was close."

"Very," I said.

"Um, Mister," the cab driver said, "Where are we going now?"

I gave him the address to the private hangar for our chartered plane. "We're heading home," I said.

Ace looked at me in surprise. "What about our business in Switzerland?"

"It's been aborted," I said. "Change of plans. Cover's blown, Ace. We have to head home."

Ace looked lost for a second.

"Don't worry, Dude," I said. "We are still alive and still a step ahead of them."

"That pretty young woman," the cab driver said, "Why is she after you?"

Normally I wouldn't engage in conversations about my business with anyone when I travel, but here I felt like Ace and I needed to let out a little steam. "Lover's spat," I said. "She thought I was cheating on her."

The cab driver laughed and said, "Women. The fiery ones… so exciting, but when you get them mad, you better flee for your lives!"

Ace and I laughed at that.

Yeah, now the tables had turned. I wasn't the one going for my targets. I have become their target.

Chapter 5

<u>Parker James</u>

On the flight back to California from Switzerland, I had cut my long silver platinum hair to a stylish emo style haircut and dyed it a copper brown.

"You look like Archie from the comic strips," Ace said. The hair and those blue eyes of yours."

"Do I look different enough?" I asked, putting on some prescription-free glasses and changing from my business suit into a college nerd's clothes.

"Yes, different, alright," Ace said.

"Great, now can you put together some documents for me to have a whole new identity, Genius?"

"Sure thing," Ace said, taking out a polaroid camera to take a picture of me against the wall of the luxury jet we were in. He went to work on his laptop, while I made a few phone calls to movers.

"We need a new house," I said. "Our location's been compromised so we're no longer safe there."

"Where do you want to move?" Ace asked.

"Still near Hollywood," I said. "Near Summer's Aunt Sookie's house so I can still keep an eye on things there for the real Summer's safety. But not in Malibu."

"I'll get a realtor to help us find a place," Ace said. "What about your business? Parker James still has a business you just opened up in Los Angeles. What are you going to do about that?"

I smiled. "Simple. I'm selling it. Since opening up my business, the value has increased.

Despite what Stanley did, killing my employees and threating them, the company is still valuable, and I can find offers pretty quickly."

"You're really selling it off, after all these years?" Ace asked.

"I can't be Parker James any longer," I said. "But I can still managed to keep my business as Thad Newton, genius tech guru from the East Coast, who wanted to own a tech security company on the West Coast."

"Thad Newton," Ace said. "I like it. Fits your new look. So you're selling Parker James' business to Thad Newton?"

"Yup," I said. "Using a private sale of just stocks, Newton would own the majority of stocks versus Parker James." I sent a few text messages as

Ace continued working on changing my identity on all the sites.

We continued working on the transition as well as the move right up to the point we landed.

"The realtor found us a place in the hills. A ranch with some grape vines, too," Ace said. "Secluded with gates to get in. Perfect for a place that we can spruce up for security."

"Pictures?" I asked.

Ace showed me a few photos of the place, and I agree to take a look.

He handed me all the documents I needed to go with my new look and identity. Ace couldn't have done a better job than the best of the art forgers. All my documents looked and checked out as real.

I checked my text. My broker had came through the sale of my company to Thad Newton.

Now it was time to become Thad Newton. And to continue on my I.C. mission with a new identity.

Chapter 6

<u>Dante Black/Thad Newton</u>

"Damn," Ace said. "This new house is much better than the last one. I could stay here forever!"

"Still in Malibu, although I said not Malibu, but I agree. It was a blessing in disguise," I said. "We found a much better place after all. I really like this place, too," I took a sip from my glass of wine. "Living on a ranch growing grapes and making wine, can be my next venture," I said.

"Thank God it only took a few hours to move into since it came furnished," Ace said. "Good thinking that you had packers and a professional mover to pack up our personal things at the old house, leaving the old furniture and things we don't need there."

"Except for the Dante Black stuff in the hidden room, we had to pack up ourselves," I said. "That part was the one that took a few hours, but in the end, we were able to set up a new headquarter here at the ranch."

"Yes," Ace said, stretching. "Did I tell you how dead tire I am? Between fleeing from Switzerland and working the entire way back to the U.S. to having me pack and move all of our equipment from the old house to set up at this new house, I think I haven't stopped moving or working for almost 48 hours. I don't even know what time zone we're in anymore."

"I know, me too," I said. "Now that we've got the place wired and secured, I think we can finally relax."

I looked over at Ace, and he had already fallen asleep, lying down on the lounge chair on the patio overlooking the rolling hills, with a view of the ocean below, and the green vineyards all around. I threw a flannel throw on him, and he barely flinched. Completely knocked out and snoring.

I pulled a throw around me, relishing its softness. It wasn't too long when I drifted off to sleep lulled into a tranquil one from the sweet smell of grapes in the breeze.

When I woke up, Ace was in the kitchen, sitting at the countertop with his laptop in front of him and headphones on. "Hey," I said. "What are you listening to?"

"They're all in Worth's Office," Ace said. "Having a meeting. Summer, um, Dorothy, too."

"No, really?" I pulled up the stool next to him and sat down, putting on my headphones.

"I knew not to trust Clay Black," Worth was saying. "He was supposed to kill Dante for failing his mission. But in the end, guess Clay went soft."

"We should have had the Scarecrow go in to kill them both off, at the time," Rockefeller's gruff voice said. "But Dante Black had such a stellar record of mission completes. One hundred percent. Who knew it would be the Summer Jones mission that would screw everything up."

"He was the best of our assassins, Founder and Offsprings alike," Claire's voice said.

I cringed, hearing the raspy smoker's voice that barely sounded like a woman's. She gave me the assignment to eliminate her competition, which was the beloved head of Millions Corp. They were initially a competitor for Black Biotech, but my father Clay Black had some sense not to touch them for some reason. Max Millions, the grandson and heir to Millions Corp, whom I went to Hidden Falls High with Summer in Malibu, turned out to be a decent guy. The way he was so torn up after his grandfather died, and how it affected Summer…I guess that was the beginning of the melting of my mechanical heart. When I wanted to be someone else other than Dante Black.

It was Claire who gave me the ultimatum to take out the head of Millions Corp all on account that he had given the contract to be the sole supplier of organic produce for his health food supplements branch to Claire's competitor.

Told you she was ruthless.

"But even the best could be taken down," Claire's voice said continuing the conversation in Worth's office we had picked up on my surveillance pen audio device. "Right, Dorothy?"

"Yes, Mother," Dorothy's voice said. Gone was the sweet voice of Summer's, that was replaced by a husky female voice… Dorothy's real voice. "I could have blown his head off earlier had he not been tipped off."

Claire's voice said, "Are you saying someone from the Inner Circle tipped him off?"

"How else could he have known I would be coming for him? How else would he had figured out that I was not Summer Jones, but an imposter he had been banging all this time?" Dorothy huffed. "I'd say, Mother, some fucker within had tipped him off, and I aim to find out who!"

"Tempers tempers," Rockefeller said smoothly. "You have no proof it was one of us. For all we know, you could have tipped him off yourself. After all, dear, you did mentioned how he was so good in bed."

"Mother!" Dorothy yelled. "Did you tell them that?"

"No," Worth said, "Remember, Dorothy and Claire, we have eyes and ears everywhere. From what we've learned over the years, taught to us from Clay himself, we even watch our own very carefully."

"Especially our own," Rockefeller said.

"You should have taught your daughter better," Worth said to Claire.

"Well, let's see how your son does, Rock. And yours, Worth. I'm sure they aren't any better than my girl."

"Sure, sure!" Worth said. "Now that the word on the street is that Dante Black isn't dead, but is Parker James; all the little assassins would be itching to get him. What a prize. Dante Black, the one with no heart. The Black Heart."

"Stan's son wants first shot," Rockefeller said. "After all, Dante took out Stan so the Scarecrow wants revenge. We will grant him that, according to rules, although Dorothy had already violated that rule and went ahead to try to take the first shot."

"He was too late. Missed his chance in Hollywood," Dorothy said. "It's my turn."

"Not so fast," Worth said. "Rules are rules. Scarecrow gets a chance to revenge his parent's death from one of our own assassins. It's the privilege of being in the Inner Circle."

"So Scarecrow can get the glory?" Dorothy spatted. "Fuck that. Dante Black was putty in my hands. He adored me. He would do anything for me."

"As Summer Jones," Worth said. "Only when he thought you were Summer. It wasn't because of who you are in real life, girl. In real life, he couldn't give a fuck who you are, Dorothy."

At that, there was no response from Dorothy so I think Worth's message had gotten to her.

Claire's voice said, "At least when you were playing Summer Jones, you got to fulfill your fantasy of fucking Dante, the King of the Assassins. Glad you got that girlish nonsense out of your system and now can be a real assassin yourself."

"Okay, so Scarecrow gets his turn. If he doesn't come through, then whose turn is it?" Dorothy asked.

"Scarecrow gets assassinated himself," Worth says. "No loose ends. The one to assassinate him would get to go after Dante Black. That's the penalty for failure."

Ace gave me a look of shock. "Harsh," he said.

I nodded. I knew that penalty myself. After all, my own father came after me to assassinate me for failing to carry out my mission with Summer.

He wanted to be the one to do it rather than someone else. But instead, he let me go, where I only barely surviving the explosion that supposedly killed me and Summer, letting me to escape and go in hiding as a ghost.

"So where's Scarecrow now?" Dorothy asked.

"Want to know where your boyfriend's whereabouts now since you want to be the one to assassinate him if he fails?" Worth asked.

Dorothy laughed. "Scarecrow is my friend, my buddy, not my boyfriend. But if he fails… anyone's game."

"And he knows that game pretty well already," Rockefeller said. "Scarecrow's signal just went dead. Last time we traced him, he was still in

Hollywood. Then Malibu where you said Dante Black posing as Parker James' house was."

"We'll find out soon enough if he completes his mission or…" Worth said.

"Dorothy?" Claire's voice called out. "Where is she?"

"Must be out to catch the earliest flight back to California," Rockefeller laughed. "Bet she can't wait to see Scarecrow fail so she gets her chance to kill Dante Black. Vicious like her mother."

Claire laughed. "No one's as vicious as I am, Sirs, especially when I'm hungry. Let's get some dinner now. I saw a restaurant across from that hotel next door that I'd like to try out. Let's go there."

There was some shuffling as chairs moved, and then the closing of a door as they left Worth's office.

"Shit," I said. "That was fucking eye-opening. To think I've been carrying out their cruel orders all these years. It makes me all the more motivated to bring each of them down." I turned to Ace. "Let's see what Scarecrow is up to, shall we?"

Ace had already switched the screen to show the footage of all the CCTVs we still had on the property, which technically was still owned by Parker James. Sure enough, there was a figure in black with a gun held out in front of him, approaching the patio door of my old house. With a kick on the frame, the door opened, allowing Scarecrow to enter.

So far our plan was working. Scarecrow was inside a house that we had set up just for him.

Although we had moved most of our belongings out to our new ranch house in the hills, the rest of the house was still furnished, making it seem as though we still lived there.

Scarecrow approached the living room cautiously before heading into my bedroom. From there, he shot up the bed. "Take that, Motherfucker!" his raspy rock star voice called out. "Take that for sleeping with my girl Kathryn. Yeah, Summer to you. But to the I.C., she's Dorothy!"

Ace looked over at me and said, "He has the hots for Dorothy?"

"Complicated," I said.

"Hold on," Ace said, "let's get a close up on who this Scarecrow is…"

Ace positioned one of the cameras to get closer to Scarecrow and closer until we were looking into the face of someone very familiar. And very startled. He was looking into the camera as though he just realized he'd been caught. Without a second to lose, he bolted out of the room, out of the house, and into the night.

Ace was shaking his head. "Man, I'm so disappointed," he said. "My rock idol Rob Raven, is the Scarecrow."

He shook his head again. "The irony of it all. I should've known… Raven, um, Scarecrow? Damn!"

I patted his shoulder and said, "I missed it too. Partly because it just seemed too obvious."

"And about Dorothy being Summer..." Ace said. "I'm sorry about that. I know you wanted to be back with Summer so badly..."

"You wanted to tell me Summer wasn't my Summer, didn't you?" I said. "But you knew I wouldn't want to hear it."

Ace nodded.

"I wouldn't but, it would've cost us our lives if we haven't found out the truth," I said. I sighed. "Better to know the truth than to be dead, right?"

"Right," Ace said. "Now what?"

"We go to our next step," I said, "And hope the I.C. doesn't know anything about Thad Newton."

Chapter 7

<u>Rob Raven/Scarecrow</u>

I can deal with the shrill cries of my fans and the young women who were always chasing me and wanting a piece of me after my concerts. It came with the territory as a rock star, as did me having to be a fucking assassin just because my father was part of a messed up secret world-domination organization known as the Inner Circle.

All these years, I had been building up my career as a musician, only to have to suddenly become an assassin and to go on a mission that was near impossible...to take down the elusive and legendary Dante Black, who at age 17 was already a legend within the Inner Circle and its partners.

The guy apparently died, too. And like a phoenix rising from the ashes, he suddenly reappeared. Surprised all of us, and fucking took out my asshole of a father.

Now rules were rules. Instead of some other assassin going after him, I have to be the one so I could get my revenge. It was a privilege reserved for the family of an Inner Circle Founder. But it was a privilege I never asked for, nor did I wanted. To tell the truth, I was happy just being Rob Raven.

Until you put Kathryn in the picture…the little French girl who I became friends with over the years from the Inner Circle. Geeky gawky me was no match for the athletic beauty she was at age 12 when I first met her. It was because she beat me in wrestling that my father decided to up my training to become a lean mean fighting machine. Thanks to her, I bulked up and was now a lethal weapon.

And thanks to her, posing as Dante Black's love of his life Summer Jones, I knew where his house was. Not too far from mine, but it seemed like he was thousands of miles away. No one was home.

Not only that, I fucking got myself caught on camera, and I knew he was watching me. Fuck! Fuck! Fuck!

I only have one chance to get him, to take him out or I would be taken out. It was him or me, and I'd rather it be him.

After hightailing it out of his compound, I had to regroup. Figure out my next move.

Dante Black already took out Stanley. His next targets would either be Worth, Rockefeller, or Claire. Which one would it be?

I pulled out my phone and punched in a number.

"Hello, Darling," a husky voice said. Kathryn.

"What are you doing, Babe," I asked.

"Flying back to the States," she said.

"From where?" I asked.

"Europe, Darling," she purred. "It's so pretty here at this time of the year."

"Tired of being in sunny California pretending to be a beach girl?" I asked Kathryn, who I knew was the opposite of a beach girl in reality. She'd rather spend all day trying out the latest fashions than anywhere on the surf.

"You know me too well," she laughed. "I miss my champagne, my caviar, and everything decadent."

"That's my girl," I said. "It's too bad we didn't hang out more when I saw you at my concert."

"Well, I had my job to do," she said.

"And a very good job you did, too," I said, gritting my teeth. "Total transformation. You underwent plastic surgery everywhere to look just like Summer Jones. And you changed your voice to sound like her. You sure had him fooled, didn't you?"

"I would like to think so," Kathryn said. "He never suspected."

"So, Babe," I said, "Where do you think he is?"

"Your guess is as good as mine," she said.

"But you know him so much better than I do, having been with him, talked to him…"

"And fucked with him," she laughed. "Yes, most of the time we were together we just kept fucking. Couldn't get enough of it. The man is so well-hung, so luscious. What he could do with his tongue. I had the most orgasms I've ever had."

I nearly punched the window of my car as I sat, parked in front of Parker James' tech company's building. "Would you miss being fucked by him?" I asked.

She sighed. "It would be a shame to have to take out one of the hottest lovers the world had ever had, but…"

"Don't worry, Kathryn," I said clenching my fist. "You don't have to take him out. I will."

And I will take Dante Black down, now that I knew how Kathryn was so taken by him. I didn't need the competition, plus, yeah, if I didn't take him down, I might as well dig my own grave now.

So I waited and waited in my car until I saw someone walk out of Parker James' building. One of his top executives. I think his name was Jeremy Rollins. Dante Black seemed to care about his employees. I learned that from seeing how my own father got to Dante when he sent him the head of one of his employees to him at his home.

If I can't find Dante by looking for him, I'll get him to come to me.

Chapter 8

<u>Dante Black/Thad Newton</u>
New York

"This is a nice change of pace," Ace said as we got settled into our two-room suite at the Belvedere Grand Hotel near Wall Street.

"New York had always been more to my pace than California," I said. "But it grew on me."

"Because of Summer," Ace said.

"I would live anywhere she lived," I said.

"Well, then, why are we here in New York at such a short notice, Boss?" Ace asked. "We literally took the red eye out to get here this morning."

"The sale of Parker James' company to Thad Newton would be final today, and I'm here to sign some papers."

"Good to know," Ace said.

"There will be an announcement in the papers, too," I said.

"Everything is moving as planned," Ace smiled as he set up his operations on the dining table in our suite. "When do you think you'll have papers signed and all that Parker James business done by?"

"By lunchtime," I said. "Should go smoothly."

"Good," Ace said. "By then, I should be able to cut into the system and set up a distraction."

"Yes, I'll leave you to it," I said, getting dressed in a suit and combing my copper hair in place. I put on my glasses, grabbed a thin silver briefcase and headed out just as my phone began ringing.

"Hello?" I said, picking up my phone. "Theo? Yes, I'm ready to sign the papers at your office. I'll be there in about ten minutes."

It was a nice brisk walk from the hotel to my business broker's office in the Wall Street area of New York. I picked up a large pizza along the way and entered the nice steel and chrome building where Theo had his office. It wasn't something Parker James did. It definitely wasn't something Dante Black would do. But for Thad Newton, being spontaneous, a bit eccentric, and nerdy, was something he would do.

I walked in carrying the large box of pizza, into the building, one I had previously set up a system, partially. It was Rockefeller's own building. In the lobby was a metal detector and body scanner where I had to empty all the contents of my pockets and place my briefcase on a belt. The pizza box was too large to fit onto the belt, and too tall for the scanner so I handed it to the nice lady who was waiting on the other side to hold. After I went through and fixed my belt and grabbed my metal objects, the lady handed me my pizza box, and I ran into the elevator going up. The pizza soon filled the elevator with the aroma of fresh baked pizza. "Oh, that smells so good," the woman in the elevator said next to me.

"Guido's Pizza," I said. "Down the street."

"That's where I'll go for lunch," she said. "Thanks for the suggestion."

"No problem," I smiled, adjusting my glasses.

She smiled at me, licking her lips. I didn't know if she wanted a piece of the pizza now or if she wanted a piece of Thad Newton. If it was Parker James or Dante Black, it would be more obvious.

"Cute haircut," she said.

"Thanks," I said, looking down, acting shy, very Thad-like.

"Where are you heading with the pizza?" she asked.

"Oh, I had to pick up the pizza for a small office party," I said.

"Okay," she said. I heard her stomach growl.

"Sorry," I would offer you a slice, but my boss would be mad at me if she found any piece missing."

"I understand," she said. "Nope, I'll just go get myself one slice at Guido's."

"Again, sorry about that," I said.

"No problem," she said. "And if I see you again, my name's Alice. I work for Mr. Rockefeller, himself. The guy who owns this building." She took out her card and handed it to me. "If you need anything in this building, just call me."

"Oh, that's really sweet of you," I said. "Thank you, Alice. I will!"

The elevator stopped, and Alice got off, leaving me to stop at the next floor, where Theo's office was. I walked into his office and closed the door. I shook my head…so that was Rockefeller's secretary, Alice. Ace and I already had tapped into her computer to get into Rockefeller's schedule. We were very well-acquainted with her computer. So now I knew how she looked like, too. Not quite as young and buxom like Worth's secretary Anna, but not bad, either.

"Hey, nice change," Theo said in his deep voice as I walked into my broker's office. "I could barely recognize you with that copper hair and glasses. But nerdy boyish fits you, too, Dante."

Yes, he was one of the handful of people besides Ace who knew I was Dante.

He came over to fist bump me and give me a hug. "How are you doing, Bro?" I asked.

"Good," Theo said.

"Like your new office here?" I asked.

"Great view," Theo said, "No complaints."

"So it's been like, what, six months since you moved in," I asked.

"About," Theo said. "Six months of watching and observing."

I handed him a card. "Know who this is?" I asked.

"Yes, Alice Kopowsky," he said. "Nice lady. She works for Rockefeller himself. His secretary."

"Just met her, myself," I said. "Seems she's very accessible and friendly. Lonely, however.

Could use some company. Might be someone we can cozy up to."

"Got it," Theo said. "Oh, the paperwork went through no problem on the transfer of ownership. And the press already has the story."

"So now Parker James has headed back to England, and Thad Newton is the new Boss," I said.

I put the box of pizza down and opened it.

Theo's face broke out into surprise. "Wow, you came prepared."

"Yup," I said. Hidden under the pizza was a gun, a few surveillance tools, and a knife. "Here are the tools for you," I said, handing them over to him. "The gun's mine, and so's the knife."

"Pizza any good?" Theo asked.

I took a slice and bit into it. "Very."

"Alrighty, then," Theo grinned, taking a slice and biting into it. "Real good."

I finished mine and ate another slice.

A text came through on my phone from Ace.

ACE: All's set. You're free to roam.

I looked down at my smartwatch and pressed a button. I was tapped into the feed of the camera in front of Rockefeller's office.

"Theo, it's rock n' roll time," I said, putting on a baseball cap, a messenger's jacket, and taking off my glasses.

Theo walked with me down the stairwell to the floor below where Alice had gotten off and walked over to place a mirror over another camera in the hallway.

At Rockefeller's Office, I walked in, holding a delivery box covering my gun prepared to take out Rockefeller, but he wasn't at his desk, as I thought.

I placed the delivery box on his desk and slapped an audio surveillance device onto the side of his desk.

Theo popped his head into the office and said, "Hurry. Someone's coming up the elevator."

I heard a flush of a toilet from the bathroom in Rockefeller's office and gritted my teeth. Rockefeller was in there. Should I wait and get him now or abort?

Theo whispered. "Coming down the hallway."

I walked out of the office and out into the hallway, slipping into an alcove along the hallway with Theo.

We headed down the stairwell and into his office where I changed into my business suit again.

"That was close," Theo said. "It's too bad you couldn't carry out your…"

Ace was calling me. "Listen to this," he said.

He began playing an audio feed of someone coughing. Then choking. It came from the audio surveillance device I planted on Rockefeller's desk.

"That's Rockefeller," I said.

"Help!" Rockefeller yelled hoarsely. Then there was a big thud.

Ace whistled. "Whatever you did, you did it, Boss."

Theo whistled too. "I thought we had aborted the mission. But you had one more card up your sleeve, didn't you, Boss?"

"Yes, an old cold war spy trick my father taught me, which I've used a few times before," I said. "I'm surprised Rockefeller couldn't detect it."

"I'd like to know what it was you did, but it's time to get you out of here before someone finds him," Theo said, taking the gun and knife from me. "Thanks for bringing these. I'll know what to do with these."

"That's why I brought it. I can count on you. Always, Bro." I gave him a hug and said, "Thanks, Theo. Great seeing you again."

"Anytime, Boss," Theo said. "Anytime."

I walked out of his office and out of the building, like nothing had ever happened.

Chapter 9

<u>Scarecrow</u>

I was too late.

Not only had Dante Black eluded me from my search for him, but he wasn't even in town when I left a note for him at his building's receptionist desk.

"I have your Head of Security, Parker. Come and get him." – Scarecrow.

Turned out he was no longer owner of the building, too. Nor was he the owner of his company so all I did was in vain. The news was all over it.

Some geeky guy named Thad Newton had bought his company overnight.

He wouldn't even know who the Head of Security was. Nor would he care.

My phone started ringing, and I picked up. It was Kathryn.

"Hey," she said. "I'm back in California. Where are you?"

"Hey Babe," I said. "I'm at my place."

"I'll swing by. I've got some goodies from Europe I want to share with you," she cooed.

Boy, she sounded so sexy then. "Goodies! Yeah, Babe, that's what I'm talking about. Come on by, and we'll just hang. Just you and me."

"I'll be there in an hour," she said.

"See you in a bit," I said. I got up and walked over to my garage. I didn't mean to keep the Head of Security there, but I didn't know where else to keep him.

He had his hands tied behind his back and a hood over his head. I placed him in my Porsche and took off. "Hey," he said. "Is there anything I can help you with? I can give you information about the company. I can…"

"Save it," I said.

"You kidnapped me for a reason, didn't you?" he asked.

"Your information means nothing to me now," I said. "As of today, someone else owns the company you work for. I don't need information from you anymore. You're no longer leverage for me."

"Oh no no no no!" the man cried.

I stopped the car and took him out of the car.

The man began peeing all over himself. I felt sick.

"You don't have to do this," he said.

I faced him away from me, and I heard him sobbing.

"Shit, you know," I said. "You better not tell anyone about this. You promise? If you do…"

"I swear I won't," he said. "I swear!"

I cut open his ropes and took off his hood and pushed him forward. "You are free to go!"

He fell forward to the ground and started crying, "Thank you! Thank you!"

I quickly took off in my car before he could see who I was. At least if I was going to go down in flames, I wouldn't be taking an innocent with me on my conscience. In that way, I was very different from my father. And if I had a choice, I would never belong to some screwed up organization like the Inner Circle in the first place.

As Rob Raven would tell his fans, "Live and Let Live and most importantly, Rock On!"

Chapter 10

<u>Kathryn/Dorothy</u>

I drove slower than I normally would going to Rob Raven's house.

He had a mansion in the Hollywood Hills that would befit any rock star. About 10,000 square feet with 5 bedrooms and 7 bathrooms along with a six-car garage; his house was as large as any of my mother's estates in the countryside of France. Of course, it had a completely different vibe.

One that was refreshingly different from Mom's stuffy old-world taste. Where Mom's chateaus were hundreds of years old, Rob's mansion was brand new, modern contemporary, and very masculine.

Not quite my style, but again, it was different.

Just like my friendship with Rob was different. He was a friend, but he wasn't in that you could never really have friends when you're in the Inner Circle. You couldn't even trust your own parents. Or your kids. If I would ever live long enough to have kids.

Which I probably wouldn't have anyways, because if I do live long enough, it would mean I would still be part of the Inner Circle and that would mean my kids would be assassins, too. And so the cycle continues.

So… I was taking my time getting over to Rob's house… with my goodies that would make him die with a smile on his face. Or I hope.

Chapter 11

<u>Rob Raven/Scarecrow</u>

Despite how big my pad was, I only had one housekeeper who would come in during the day to clean and leave in the afternoon to go home. No one else lived in my house except me. But being the rock star that I was, I constantly had people over. My manager, band mates, their girls, groupies…

But tonight everyone was gone. The house was empty except for me because Kathryn was coming over.

The entire thing with her having a steamy affair with Parker James, fucking everyday, had my blood boiling. Undercover work or not, Kathryn was mine…the girl I had a crush on for years. No groupies, no girlfriends I've ever had came close to what I felt for her. Only she never knew it.

So when I opened the door to let Kathryn into my pad, I was blown away by what I saw.

"Hello, Robbie Baby," she purred. Gone was her long caramel hair that resembled Summer's. Gone was her Barbie-doll-like nose and beautiful hazel eyes.

"Kathryn?" I asked. "Is that you?"

She laughed her husky laugh. "Of course, Babe," she said. "Just had some work done so I'm no longer Summer. No longer the Kathryn you remember seeing too, but an entirely new look."

She played with her chin-length bobbed and banged black hair, blinked her almond-shaped brown eyes, and twirled around. Her shapely body was wrapped in black latex. She blew me a kiss from her bright red lips. "Like it?"

She looked exotic. Sexy as hell, and yeah, a dominatrix.

"Looking hot," I mumbled.

"Glad you liked it," she said, sauntering into my house on six-inch heels, closing the door behind her. "I needed a change from the goody Victoria Secret model look that was all Summer Jones to something completely different," she said. She walked over to me to give me a big hug before pulling away. "Are we alone?"

"Yes," I said, my voice husky with need. Her hug was enough to get me hard as her breasts crushed against my chest.

"Good," she whispered into my ear. "I need you to help me."

"With what?" I asked.

"To practice my new identity on… to perfect it," she said.

"And who are you supposed to be now?" I asked.

"Betty Boop," she laughed. "Only an Asian American version and a fucking hot dominatrix."

"My God," I groaned. "You're pulling it off for me right now."

"Good," she leaned over to run her fingertip over my cheeks and then my lips. "You're the one I always wanted to practice my dominatrix fantasy on."

I gulped then swallowed. "Really?"

"Yeah," she purred. "I never told you, but you being a rock star and turning on all your fans on stage with how you grind your hips, singing in that raspy hot voice of yours, had always turned me on."

"What do you want to do about it?" I asked, pulling her to me with my arm around her tiny waist so she could feel my hard-on against her.

"I want to act out my fantasy with you," her lips hovered over mine.

"About time," I crushed my lips over hers, kissing her with all the pent-up desire I had for her.

My tongue delved into her sweet mouth, tangling with hers until she was moaning. "Take me to your bed," she moaned. "Now."

"My pleasure," I growled, lifting her light frame and wrapping her legs around my waist as I carried her through the living room, up the stairs, and into my huge bed. I laid her down gently on it, before I began unzipping my pants.

"Hold on," she said, her eyes trained on my crotch as she sat up. "I'll undress you." She wagged her finger at me to come over, which I obliged.

When I came up to her hands, she unzipped me, reached into my boxers and pulled out my rock hard dick. "Ooooh!" she cried out delightedly. "Had I known you were this big, I would have been fucking you years ago." She took me into her mouth, deeper and deeper, until my root was to her lips.

"Fuck!" I groaned as she sucked me in and out, licking me, sucking me until I came so quickly and hard that she almost gagged. I pulled out, and she looked up at me, swallowing before she wiped her mouth.

"That was good!" she laughed.

"Fucking good!" I laughed with her. "What do you want to do next?"

She got up and undressed the rest of me, pulling off my t-shirt and my pants. "Get on the bed," she order.

I sat down in bed and laid down. She sat down next to me then pulled my arms up, handcuffing them to the headboard. She got off the bed and said, "Now for the real fun."

She walked over to my closet and came out with one of my belts, a silver chain-linked one that had a massive diamond buckle. It was one I wore during one of my concerts. "Oh, this one is a real blingy," she said. "I remembered you wearing this with a skintight pair of leather chaps. Hot."

She came over, ran the belt against my thighs to my inner thigh before she slapped it harder on my chest. "Ouch!" I yelled.

"No pain, no gain," she growled. She came over, unzipping her latex suit until she was buck naked, showing her full round D-cup breasts, smooth and tight body, her tiny waist, large round butt, and long legs.

"You're so beautiful," I said.

She grinned, "I always knew you had a thing for me, Robbie. Now you've earned your chance to be with me."

She sat on top of me before positioning her pussy near my rod. She was wet and sliding against it, before she slid down completely on me. Once on top of me, she went wild, going up and down on me while her hands went to her breasts to pinch her own nipples. "Yes, yes, so fucking good!"

"Ride me, Baby," I groaned.

"Like a cowgirl on a bucking stallion," she squealed. She took out a long bandana and held it over my face. "Close your eyes. You'll enjoy this part much more if you do."

"Okay," I went along with her. "But fuck, I'm gonna come really soon!"

"That's what I'm hoping for!" she said, as she kept riding me.

"I'm about to…"

"Then you'll enjoy this goody I have for you!" She tied the bandana around my neck tightly.

For a moment, I thought she was going to choke me to death, but she eased off, smiled at me sweetly, and then said, "I've always liked you. You were the only decent one in the group. Dante, he was way above us, kept away from the rest of us Offsprings so I never got to know him. But you, Lion, and Wizard were like family, you know."

The bandana she held against my neck began tightening and tightening as she moaned and began shuddering with her oncoming climax. I began shuddering, as I felt the first of my cum squirting.

"I'm coming!" I croaked.

"Feel how good this feels then!" she pulled the bandana around my neck so tight, I could no longer breathe, as I came hard in her, feeling the most sexual high I've ever had, but also like I was dying.

My eyes began rolling backward as I tried to get my hands free from the handcuffs, but I was stuck. I was her prisoner.

With one last tug of her bandana, Kathryn stared down at me with contempt, "You failed your mission to kill Dante Black, Scarecrow. Now you are eliminated."

I felt a sharp intense pain before my brain gave out. Then nothing.

Chapter 12

<u>Kathryn/Dorothy</u>

I cleaned up every trace of my presence from Rob's prone body and his bed, his room, his house. His eyes were staring straight up like he had died having BDSM sex. With a light dusting of drugs on his lips, it looked like he had taken drugs, too.

Typical way to go for a rock star. So fitting of an ending for Rob Raven, the Scarecrow.

"Hey Mom," I pulled out my phone as I entered my car and sat down. "Scarecrow failed his mission so he was eliminated. Now it's my turn to go after Dante Black, isn't it? Isn't that how it worked?"

"Oh, Darling," Mom said. "Did you go all the way to California again just to get Scarecrow out of your way? You shouldn't have gone through the trouble. Lion is now the one who has privilege to go after Dante."

"What?" I asked. "Why?"

"Haven't you heard?" Mom said. "Rockefeller was murdered. Poisoned. No trace of it, however, and no trace of who could have done it, But we at the Inner Circle knew. Dante Black. So, Lion, now has the privilege to go after him to revenge his father."

"But I got rid of Scarecrow who was after Dante," I whined. "It's my turn!"

"No!" Mom snarled over the phone. "You will not go after him when Lion is involved. It's his privilege. Rules are rules!"

"But Mom!" I whined again.

"Enough!" Mom yelled into the phone. "You will obey the rules, Kathryn or I will come out there to eliminate you myself. You hear me?"

I stopped talking. No doubt Mom would not hesitate to kill me herself. "Okay," I said. "Lion gets his turn," I said. "Then I'll get mine!"

Epilogue

<u>Dante Black/Thad Newton</u>

Ace and I were back at my new Malibu ranch, listening in on a conversation at Rockefeller's office.

"It's my turn to go after that bastard Dante for you, Dad," a young man was saying. "The I.C. sent me word I have the sole privilege to take him down. I will, Dad or my name isn't Lion."

Ace turned to me and said, "So now, Lion's going to go after you. First Scarecrow and now Lion."

"It's to be expected," I said. "Inner Circle rules."

"What about Scarecrow?" Ace asked. "His trail went cold after he attempted to assassinate you at our old house."

"Guess he's out of the picture," I said. "One less Offspring to worry about."

"Hey, wait," Ace said. "I just got an update on news from my favorite personalities. Rob Raven's social media just went wild. Oh fuck! No way!"

"What, Ace? What's going on?" I asked walking up to him to look at his computer.

"Look! Ouch, that's bad," Ace said. "Rob Raven was found dead handcuffed to his bed after some wild bondage sex. He was also high. His mouth was full of powder." He shook his head. "I thought he was clean, but man, he was just like other rock stars."

I let Ace have a moment to grieve his favorite rocker before I said, "He probably was."

"Huh?" Ace asked. "He being on drugs would explain why he wasn't so good of an assassin as Scarecrow. He abandoned his mission after all."

"No, Ace," I said. "Someone from the I.C. took him out. Eliminated. Looks like someone really wanted to go after me for the kill instead of anyone else. And I think I know who it is."

"Are you going to take him out then?" Ace asked.

"No, but I know who I'm going to take down next in the Inner Circle. I think I'm going to play around with the minds of the Offsprings and the Founders a bit. It will make all my years of sacrifice worth it."

*****

Dante's story will continue in Book 3 of The Inner Circle Series.

The Lion (Inner Circle #3)

Scarecrow (The Inner Circle #2)

READ about Dante Black's Beginning Here:

The Hidden Falls High Series

USA TODAY BESTSELLING SERIES
HIDDEN FALLS HIGH
4-Books Box Set (Books .5 to 3)
KAILIN GOW

Scarecrow (The Inner Circle #2)

Now that Nat Donovan had left...

Hidden Falls High has a new King...

Dante Black, the blackest of the Blacks.

Another home, another new school.

Another target.

Life was supposed to be smooth sailing when you're at the
end of your high school year.

Of course it is.

Especially when you're the one your father relies on to take
care of loose ends. And by the time you're 17, you've
already earned yourself a reputation amongst the Inner
Circle as someone to be feared.

Who am I? I'm the charming Prince, the Golden Boy, the
one no one suspects to have no heart.

Until I saw her...my target. The girl I will bring down
because she is his crush. Summer.

Kailin Gow

Who knew crushes could be so cruel?

*****

There is someone new living in the Donovans' old mansion
in Hidden Falls, the exclusive enclave in Malibu. He's a
senior at the Academy, but he seems older like he's already
seen so much in the world. Maybe he has. Maybe he's not
of this world.

I thought I had finally found peace at Hidden Falls
High...but the nightmare is just beginning...

***Hidden Falls High is a Dark High School Romance
mature YA/New Adult series intended for 17 and up due to
language and mature matters. Any sex is consensual.
Another home, another new school.

More Books like The Inner Circle

BOOK SERIES

BAD BOY ROYALS OF KINGSBURY PREP (Complete)

RH New Adult/High School Bully Dark Contemporary Romance – HEAT 4 out of 5

Tempest and The Black Envelope (Books 1 and 2) with Bonus and Clue on the Treasure
https://www.amazon.com/dp/B07Z44T1PF

Revenge
https://www.amazon.com/gp/product/B07SQP3HL3

Secret Princess
https://www.amazon.com/dp/B07YLHJ38K

Fallen Royals
https://www.amazon.com/dp/B07XXC625K

Reign of Rebels
https://www.amazon.com/dp/B07XM3FKW6

Link to Kingsbury Prep Series
https://www.amazon.com/gp/bookseries/B07S7ZVZWQ

Complete Series Box Set
https://www.amazon.com/gp/product/B08781CS94

<u>Kingmakers of Kingsbury Series</u>
RH Bully Fantasy Paranormal Shifter Fae
Romance – HEAT 4 out of 5
Long before there was an All-Royals Academy called Kingsbury Prep, there was the Kingmaker and her kings.

As Violet Kingsbury, I was born to be a kingmaker. In a time when wars were common and thrones were fought after, the only name that could bring about peace...the only man that could trump the decrees of kings was Kingsbury. The Kingmaker. But when the legendary Kingmaker is disposed, and the time of the Choosing has come, can I, the daughter

of The Kingmaker rise to take the place of my father? I am about to find out as the strongest, most capable, and most legendary princes across the lands come to challenge me for the Choosing including 4 of the most handsome princes who not only wants to win, but to want to win me, too:
Avery
Axel
Reggie
Ollie

*Becoming Kingmaker, even as The Kingmaker's daughter, will not be easy in a male world where ladies were supposed to be daMs.els who needed saving. To become Kingmaker, I will prove to all, especially the princes, that I am here to stay, and will be the one doing the saving. **Kingmakers of Kingsbury Series, is a Reverse Harem Bully Romance with mixed genres elements, action, and mature scenes recommended for age 17 and up.*

Kingmaker's Kings (Book 1)
https://www.amazon.com/dp/B082QMNCW4
Kingmaker's Kiss (Book 2) (May 18, 2020)
https://www.amazon.com/gp/product/B084BZYW28

Kingmaker's Kill (Book 3) (July 28, 2020)
https://www.amazon.com/gp/product/B084BT8154

HEARTBREAK FALLS

**RH Bully Dark New Adult/High School Romance
Mystery – HEAT 4 out of 5**

With a name like Heartbreak Falls, one didn't expect to find love at the new town I had moved to courtesy of my new stepfamily aka Mom's new husband and his sons.

Something was up with my new rich stepfather, his sons, and what happened to their last stepmother. Something was up with the entire town, which my

123

stepfamily seem to run. Along with the school where my stepbrothers reigned as cruel princes. All 3 of them were known as The Heartbreakers. Two were twins and my age, and then there was Tristan, the oldest. Gorgeous but god-awful hateful to me. What was up? I was about to find out...if I lived long enough.
***Heartbreak Falls is a RH Dark Bully Romance and mystery for 18 and up. It is YA/NA and has themes of bullying and sex. If that's fine with you, then dig in! Bully Me Not is book 1 of 5 and contains a cliffhanger.*
Bully Me Not
https://www.amazon.com/dp/B07XNQV36Q

Break Me Not
https://www.amazon.com/dp/B07XX7HZZZ

Dare Me Not
https://www.amazon.com/dp/B07Z4369V7

Destroy Me Not (June 29, 2020)
https://www.amazon.com/gp/product/B084C143VR

Love Me Not (September 28, 2020)
https://www.amazon.com/gp/product/B084BTRVYN

Link to All Series
https://www.amazon.com/gp/bookseries/B07Y6PZ57G

UNSAFE HAVEN – Coming Soon!

My name is Haven Hillshire. They say that what doesn't kill you will make you stronger. During the last semester of my junior year at an elite academy in New York City, I was almost killed as a result of a bet. Three of the most gorgeous and popular boys at the Academy was suddenly interested in me. Now I know why, and I will get my revenge...as long as I don't lose my heart. **Unsafe Haven is part of the Heartbreak Falls Series, a Reverse Harem New Adult Dark Romance for age 18 and up.

HOUSE

RH Dark College New Adult Romance – HEAT 5 out of 5

It was his last will and testament.

For one week, four of us was to live together. Play nice to each other like we used to when we were kids.

Seb, Thomas, Ashford and me.

Scarecrow (The Inner Circle #2)

Three of Mr. Keystone's sons and me, the maid's daughter.

All those years, the three sons bullied and ridiculed me because I was the maid's daughter.

So, why was I back? Why did I cared to be in the same house as those three tormentors?

Because I was in Mr. Keystone's will.

He had always been kind to me, even if his sons weren't, so I could only honor his wishes. And he was like a father to me, and didn't treat me like the maid's daughter. But as soon as I could, I left to go to college. Two years ago. Meanwhile, the boys went their separate ways, too. Estranged from each other.

So why was I here having to live in the same house with his sons for a week?

I don't know, but I'm about to find out, even if it meant my old adolescent feelings for all three of them might surface again. And if being in the mansion we called a house together might jog some memories of the wild nights we've had here.

It's just one week. I could survive that. Or could I?

***House is the first book in The House Series, which is a*

Reverse Harem Dark College Romance recommended for age 18+ due to mature themes.

House (The House Series, Book #1) (May 26, 2020)
https://www.amazon.com/gp/product/B0863Z36S5

Haven (The House Series, Book #2) (August 25, 2020)
https://www.amazon.com/gp/product/B087BFJWK5
Habit (The House Series, Book #3) (Nov. 2, 2020)
https://www.amazon.com/gp/product/B087B6MZDM
HEIRS (The House Series, Book #4) (Feb. 8, 2021)
https://www.amazon.com/gp/product/B087BCKS27
Haunt (The House Series, Book #5) (April 6, 2021)
https://www.amazon.com/gp/product/B087BGL27P
Home (The House Series, Book #6) (Nov, 2021)

FALLEN FAE ACADEMY

RH Bully Romance Fantasy Paranormal Fae – HEAT 4 out of 5

"At Fallen Fae Academy, the magic will either complete you or kill you."

My name is Harley, as in Harlequin. Plucked from my home from Las Vegas, NV, and placed into an University on an arts scholarship, suddenly I am the girl the four hottest and most popular boys have decided to "initiate".

This is no ordinary "hazing" ritual, and these boys are no ordinary boys.

This mysterious University looks like any ivy league campus, but it isn't. Step in and you are transported beyond your wildest imagination. I should be ecstatic being here. Except surviving "Initiation" is going to take everything I've got.

Don't let the beauty of the four fae boys fool you. They are as dangerous as they are beautiful. And underneath everything, runs a deep secret. One I need to find out before Initiation kills me.

They think a human is weak. They think I shouldn't be at this university. I'm about to prove them wrong.

**The Fallen Fae Series is a 6-book RH Academy College Bully Romance Series featuring a badass heroine, four deadly, striking fae princes, heart-pounding action, super steamy love scenes, and great romance.

Initiation: Year 1 Fallen Fae Academy Book 1
https://www.amazon.com/Initiation-Year-Academy-Reversed-Paranormal-ebook/dp/B07V9L8LHD

Scarecrow (The Inner Circle #2)

Transformation: Year 2 Fallen Fae Academy Book 2
https://www.amazon.com/dp/B07WWFXVCH

Declaration: Year 3 Fallen Fae Academy Book 3
https://www.amazon.com/gp/product/B07XLMS.GDJ

Interruption War Year 3 (Fallen Fae Academy #4) (April 13, 2020)
https://www.amazon.com/dp/B0833JC8YJ

paperback version
https://www.amazon.com/Interruption-War-Year-Reversed-Paranormal/dp/B086Y5JYZG

Disruption (Fallen Fae Academy #5) (July 13, 2020)
https://www.amazon.com/dp/B084DB7F1B

Succession (Fallen Fae Academy Book #6) (October 19, 2020)
https://www.amazon.com/dp/B084D4VRCY

Fallen Fae Academy Box Set Part 1 (Books 1 -3)
https://www.amazon.com/gp/product/B08772LQFT

FALLEN FAE B. I. Series

RH Paranormal Romance Fantasy – HEAT 4 out of 5

Fae-ther Issues (Fallen Fae B.I. Book #1) Coming in 2021!

Now that it is changeling Harley's Ms.ion to find and capture the rogue dark fae her evil father has unleashed into the human world, Harley leaves the opulence of her mother's kingdom in the Faery RealMs. to return to her human adopted parents' home in Las Vegas to start her career as a trainee FBI agent. Piece of cake, isn't it, especially since she has finally discovered and mastered the powerful fae magic she went through the Fallen Fae Academy to learn. When a series of unusual murders show up along the Strip, and a close friend becomes the suspect, Harley would never have guess who would show up to give her some advice and clue to solve the murders…her evil dark fae wizard father. But could she trust him? Meanwhile the four princes from her Fallen Fae Academy days grapple with her decision to live in Las Vegas instead of assuming the throne of her kingdom in the Faery RealMs.

Fae-mous (Fallen Fae B.I. Book #2) (March 2021)

Harley's last case took her from casino to casino along the Las Vegas Strip in search of a killer who may have been a rogue dark fae, who wield a power she had yet to encounter. With the aid of her former classmates and still current lovers from Fallen Fae Academy, Harley devise a scheme to lure out the killer. Things become complicated when Harley and her guys discover the unusual murders before were a mere distraction from a bigger plot, her father and the rogue dark fae minions he had unleashed, had planned and had already set into motion…one that involves Las Vegas' former past as an Atomic bomb testing site to the beginning of the Apocalypse.

Fae-ful (Fallen Fae B.I. Book #3) (May 2021)

The clock is ticking. Harley and her guys must figure out the clues where the rogue dark fae army will unleash their dark magic and destroy the human race. Using the powers of all the kingdoMs. in the faery realMs., Harley and her four fae princes' powers converge to fight the power of the dark fae in the fight of their lifetimes.

<u>CRUEL PRINCES OF WYVERN ALL-BOYS ACADEMY</u>

(RH Bully Romance Fantasy Paranormal Shifters) - HEAT 4 out of 5

Enter the Wyvern All-Boys Academy as the Only Girl or Get Killed for Defying the Royal Decree

Diamonds and Dragons (Cruel Princes of Wyvern All-Boys Academy Book 1)

https://www.amazon.com/Diamonds-Dragons-Reverse-Fantasy-All-Boys-ebook/dp/B07SFV1PRH/

Roses and Emeralds (Cruel Princes of Wyvern All-Boys Academy Book 2)
https://www.amazon.com/Roses-Emeralds-Reverse-Fantasy-All-Boys-ebook/dp/B07TS1BKLT/

Silver and Starlight (Cruel Princes of Wyvern All-Boys Academy Book 3)
https://www.amazon.com/dp/B07VXVK2KV

Cruel Princes of Wyvern All-Boys Academy Complete Series Box Set
https://www.amazon.com/gp/product/B086V6ZJKH

BAD BOYS BILLIONAIRE BACHELORS CLUB (Standalone Novels)
Billionaire Romances – Heat 3 out of 5

Bidding on the Billionaire
https://www.amazon.com/gp/product/B07CB8VXFY

Movie Merger
https://www.amazon.com/gp/product/B07BX7DZ4G

Buying the Billionaire
https://www.amazon.com/gp/product/B07BXC37RQ

Broken
https://www.amazon.com/gp/product/B07BX97343

<u>VAMPIRE SAMURAI (PULSE VAMPIRE WORLD SERIES)</u>

I am Evie Everheart. As a Life's Blood Carrier, I am pursued by all vampires who want to become All Powerful or to become human again. Which is practically ALL vampires. Basically, I'm screwed.

Then I meet him, the Vampire Samurai and his band of brothers, consisting of another vampire, a fae, and a shifter. What they want of me, I've yet to find out.

Friend or foe?

I don't know. But as a carrier, all I know is that I must do everything I can to keep the vampires from getting my blood or humanity as we know it, would end.

**Vampire Samurai is a new series in the PULSE Vampires World Series, a YA/New Adult series appropriate for age 17 and up.

Vampire Samurai Vol. 1
https://www.amazon.com/gp/product/B0863PL3T2
Vampire Samurai Vol. 2
https://www.amazon.com/gp/product/B084HHV1VY

Vampire Samurai Book 3
https://www.amazon.com/gp/product/B084HHSW3Q

<u>M.A.G.E. Series</u>

Prince of Paradise
https://www.amazon.com/gp/product/B0847HFDPK

Kailin Gow's Bio

From visiting Romania, ALA YALSA Award-winning and Million-Selling Author Kailin Gow was asked to write stories about vampires; visiting the Black Forest in Germany and seeing the castles of Europe inspired her to write fantasy; visiting Asia's mystical mountains inspired her to write action adventure and mythological dystopians. From her experience in college as a peer counselor and her volunteer work with women's shelters, she was inspired to write contemporary romance with social issues for women, new adults, young adults, and teens. Having faced adversity, including battling stereotypes and bullying, Kailin Gow has become a well-known speaker and influential figure in media. Her adventurous bold spirit has taken her around the world, where she has ridden on top of elephants through jungles, hand-fed sting rays, studied kung fu from a Shaolin Temple monk, and learned cooking from a celebrity chef. She is a USA

Today Bestselling author and has been a #1 Amazon bestselling author over two-hundred times. Her Bitter Frost Series is in development as a TV Series, and her contemporary romance Loving Summer is set to become a feature film. An multi-award-winning filmmaker, director, and actress; Kailin's films have premiered at Cannes, Los Angeles, Rome, England, Paris, Korea, Japan, and even in India's Ministry of Culture.

Compelled to write her first fiction book because of 9/11, Kailin Gow now has over 400 fiction books published under Kailin Gow and various Pen Names in many genres. As a speaker and host, she has hosted international shows at the Pasadena Civic Auditorium, been a celebrity judge at beauty pageants, been a judge for writing contests, and hosted television series. She was featured as an Indie Author Success Story on the homepage of Amazon.com for a month and is also included in Amazon's book called Transformations. She is the first and only Taiwanese American to have been featured on Amazon's homepage as an Author Success Story, and the first to have sold over a million books.

She has over 50 Series, written under Kailin Gow:
***For Middle Grade (STEM Books in School) ***
Fairy Rose Chronicles - age 13 and up.
Amazon Lee Adventures Series

For 16 and up

The Frost Series
The Wolf Fey Series
The PULSE Series
FADE Series
DESIRE Series
Fire Wars Series
Alchemists Academy
Wordwick Games
Wicked Woods Series
Steampunk Scarlett
The Phantom Diaries
Stoker Sisters
Beyond Crystal River

Scarecrow (The Inner Circle #2)

Red Genesis Series
The Summer Pact

For 18 and up (New Adult/Coming of Age)
Hidden Falls High (YA/NA)
Loving Summer
The Donovan Brothers
Saving You Saving Me (You & Me Trilogy)
Never Knights
Rock Hard Musical
Shadowlight Academy (Reverse Harem Paranormal
Romance)
Shadowlight Hunters Academy (Reverse Harem
Paranormal Romance)
Society of Supernatural Sleuths (Reverse Harem
Paranormal Romance)

For 18 and up (Adult/Steamy Romance)

The Protege
Master Chefs
The Blue Room (Spin-off of Never Knights Trilogy)
The Blue Room Chronicles
Sessions
HEAT
UNassumed Series

Beautiful Girl (Standalone Novel)
The Tutor (Standalone Novel)
Rock Hard

Follow Kailin at:

@kailingow
Kailin Gow Facebook Page
http://www.facebook.com/OfficialKailinGow

Kailin Gow's Reverse Harem Reader Group
(Kailin Gow's Kingdom)
https://www.facebook.com/groups/9271670709 54766/

Kailin Gow RH Newsletter Sign Up
http://madmimi.com/signups/5d7494ecee0a46feaa 5c7a60f8f152f1/join

Bookbub
https://www.bookbub.com/authors/kailin-gow

Amazon Author Page

Scarecrow (The Inner Circle #2)

https://www.amazon.com/Kailin-
Gow/e/B002BMAEH4

Twitter
https://twitter.com/kailingow

Instagram
https://www.instagram.com/kailingow